Mater's
TREASURY OF
TALL TALES

DISNEY PRESS
New York

CONTENTS

It was a clear night in Radiator Springs. Mater and Lightning McQueen were looking up at a large full moon.
"Yep," said Mater, "I've been up there."
"PFFFT! You have not," Lightning said.

"Oh, yeah, it's real purty," Mater insisted. He began to
tell a story about the time he went to the moon. "It all
started when I was towing this car to Florida. . . ."

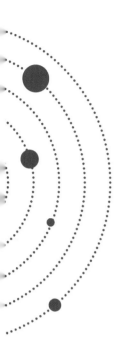

Mater described driving past Mission Control for NASCA, National Auto-Spacecraft Administration. Inside, a large monitor showed the surface of the moon. On-screen, a moon buggy named Impala Thirteen, was stuck on the edge of a crater!

"HE NEEDS A TOW!" cried one of the forklifts who worked at NASCA.

At the NASCA launch pad, other officials heard about the problem. "Where on earth are we going to get a tow?" one of them asked.

Then Roger the space shuttle saw Mater driving by. "That guy's got a tow!"

Mater agreed to help. After all, his slogan was, "No tow is too far for Tow Mater!"

Mater was whisked away for NASCA training. He had to experience maximum g-force if he was going to travel into space. A machine spun him around the room at top speed.

"WAAAAAAAAA!" Mater cried.

Soon he proved that he was ready for a mission to the moon.

The day of his flight, Mater made his way to the shuttle launchpad. He was decked out in a space suit and rocket jets. Photographers took pictures. Reporters shouted questions. Mater waved, but he didn't have time for any interviews. He rolled onto the space shuttle and strapped in.

"Welcome aboard!" said Roger as his doors shut.

Inside Mission Control, the countdown to takeoff began.
"T minus ten . . . nine . . . main engine start."

"OH, BOY!" said Mater from inside the shuttle. "I've
never been to the moon before."

"Oh, you'll love it," Roger shouted over the engine noise.

"Three . . . two . . . one!" said Mission Control.

At the base of the launchpad, smoke spilled out of the booster rockets. Then fire, followed by even more smoke.

FINALLY, BLAST OFF!

The shuttle launched into the sky.

"We have liftoff of Roger shuttle on Impala Thirteen rescue mission!" Mission Control announced.

As Roger rocketed up into space, he whooped with joy. "**WOOOOOOO-HOOOOOO!** I love my job!"

Inside the shuttle, Mater looked out the window. "See ya later, Earth."

Soon Roger's rockets had carried them deeper into space. They were approaching the moon!

"Open cargo-bay doors," Mission Control said over the radio. "Operation Tow Mater is a go!"

It was time for Mater's moon landing. He floated, weightless, out of the shuttle and into space.

"Good luck," Roger said. "See you back on Earth."

"Roger-dodger, Roger!" replied Mater.

Then the shuttle began the trip home.

The rescue mission was up to Mater now. Using his
rocket jets, he steered to the moon's surface. "Moon
Mater has landed," he said. He bounced over to Impala
Thirteen, who was still stuck.

"Connect your rescue apparatus to the frontal
structural component of the linear axle assembly,"
Impala Thirteen instructed.

"Uhh," Mater replied, "how 'bout I just give you a tow?"
He fastened his tow hook to Impala Thirteen's axle. Mater
blasted his jets and pulled the moon buggy from the crater!
"MISSION ACCOMPLISHED!" the car
said. "Now take us home!"

Mater fired his jets and rocketed toward Earth with
Impala Thirteen at the end of his towline.

In Radiator Springs, Lightning was listening carefully.

"Well, there I was," Mater was saying, "doing seventeen thousand miles an hour."

Lightning had to stop him right then. **"NO WAY!"**

"Yes, way!" Mater cried. "But that was nothin' compared to you!" He continued his story, now adding Lightning.

Lightning was flying through space wearing a bubble-top helmet and a space suit.

"**AAAHH!**" he screamed as he zoomed at top speed past Mater and Impala Thirteen.

"Watch out for reentry!" Mater called after him.

"WHAT?!" Lightning cried as he rocketed toward Earth.

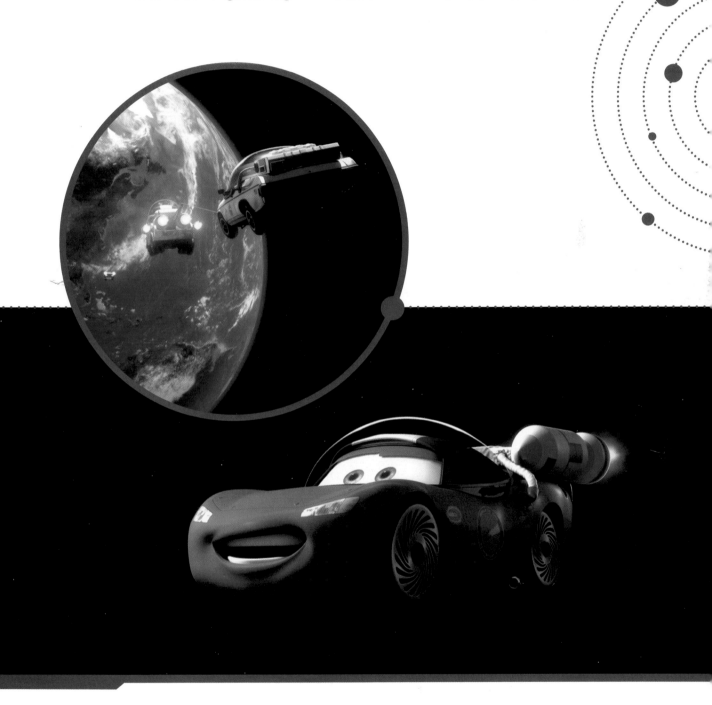

Soon, Lightning flew into the Earth's atmosphere.
Gases burned fiercely around him. *"Eee!"* He fell faster
and faster. *Splash!* He landed in cold ocean water. *Pffft!*
His parachute finally opened, although much too late.

Nearby, Mater's and Impala Thirteen's chutes carried
them gently down. Their rescue raft inflated right away.

Mater used his tow hook to lift Lightning into the raft.
"Don't worry," said Mater. **"I GOTCHA."**

Mater, Lightning, and Impala Thirteen were welcomed
back on Earth. They were honored in a big ticker-tape
parade, appeared as guests on a TV talk show, and
were on the front covers of three magazines.

In Radiator Springs, Mater had just finished his story.
"Oh, come on," Lightning said. "That did not happen."
Suddenly, Roger the shuttle set down next to them.
"Suit yourself," Mater said, and then he drove up a
ramp into the shuttle.

Lightning watched in awe as the shuttle fired up its
rockets and **LAUNCHED INTO THE AIR!**

MONSTER TRUCK MATER

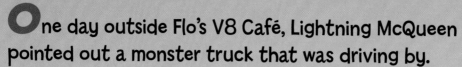

One day outside Flo's V8 Café, Lightning McQueen pointed out a monster truck that was driving by.

"I used to wrestle trucks bigger than that," Mater told him. "I used to be a monster-truck wrestler!"

Mater began to tell Lightning a story about the time he was a wrestler called the Tormentor. His first match was in a dark arena filled with cheering fans. Mater wore a blue-and-red wrestling mask.

An announcer's voice boomed out: "Introducing . . . the Tormentor!"

"'Scuse me," called Mater from inside the ring.

"THAT'S TOW MATER!"

The announcer ignored him. Instead, he introduced the Tormentor's opponent.

"THE I-SCREAMER!"

A clown-faced ice-cream truck with monster wheels rolled into the ring.

The Tormentor wasn't sure how to wrestle such a big truck. So he quickly put on a beanie cap, hoping to trick his opponent instead. "Can I have one double-dip dipstick sundae, please?"

"Huh?" said the I-Screamer. "Oh, sure."

When the ice-cream truck reached for a sundae, the Tormentor grabbed the wrestler's bumper with his tow hook and flipped him. Then the Tormentor sprayed the truck with a fire extinguisher. Now the I-Screamer looked like an ice-cream sundae!

The referee announced to the crowd that the Tormentor had won.

After his first win, the Tormentor got a new paint job.
Soon he faced Captain Collision, a military truck.
"Drop and give me twenty!" Captain Collision shouted.
Instead the Tormentor bounced off the ropes and
knocked the captain right onto his back.

"ONE . . . TWO . . . THREE,"

the referee counted. Then he declared a winner: the
Tormentor!

In his next match, the Tormentor found himself trapped in Rastacarian's dreadlock grip. "Me be jammin' now, man," the other truck taunted.

Then the Tormentor sharply yanked his opponent's hood. Rastacarian tumbled backward, and his bungee-cord dreadlocks came loose.

The referee hurried over to the Tormentor.

"THE WINNER!"

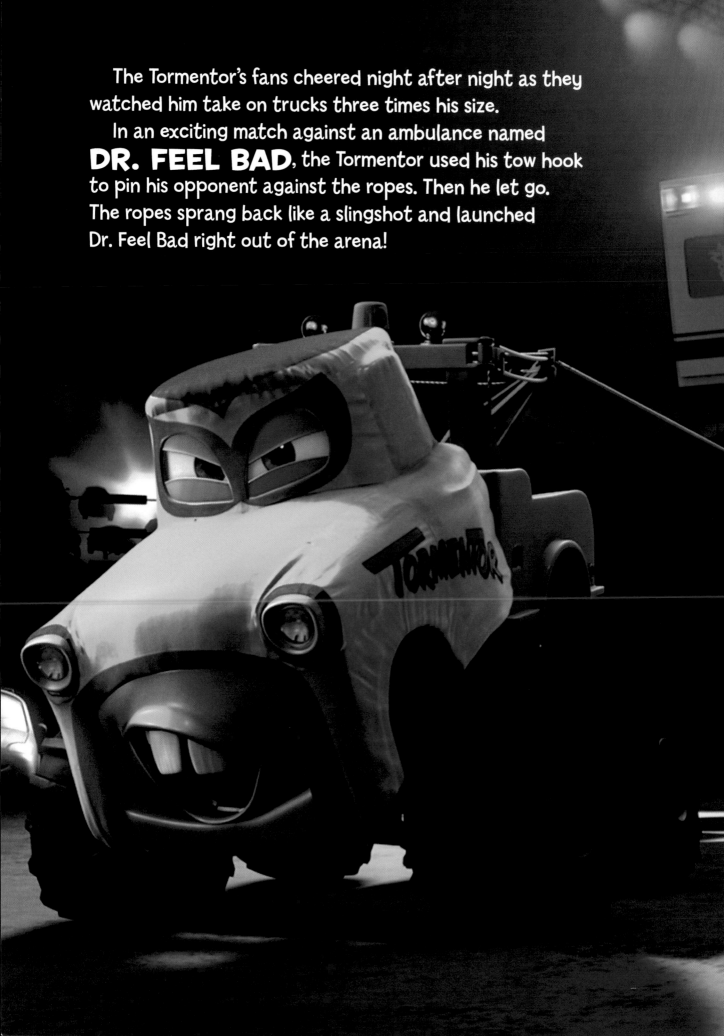

The Tormentor's fans cheered night after night as they watched him take on trucks three times his size.

In an exciting match against an ambulance named **DR. FEEL BAD**, the Tormentor used his tow hook to pin his opponent against the ropes. Then he let go. The ropes sprang back like a slingshot and launched Dr. Feel Bad right out of the arena!

In the middle of a match with **PADDY O'CONCRETE**, the Tormentor found himself backed into a corner, about to get concrete poured over him! At the last moment, the Tormentor used his tow hook to turn the mixer's chute around. The concrete dumped all over Paddy instead, and he was trapped.

"Oh-ho! He got paved!" the announcer shouted.

The Tormentor just couldn't stop winning, and soon he made it all the way to the world-championship match! The audience went wild as he rolled onto the stage. Then they booed the current champion, a very tiny car named **DR. FRANKENWAGON**.

The Tormentor laughed when he saw his opponent. Piece of cake, he said to himself. He was feeling confident until he saw . . .

. . . DR. FRANKENWAGON'S MONSTER!

Just one of the Monster's tires was bigger than the Tormentor. He had a giant scoop on one side and a claw on the other. The wrecking ball on his back could crush an average-size truck with one direct hit.

The Monster roared. He cast a frightening shadow across the wrestling ring. All of a sudden, the Tormentor felt very, very small.

Back in Radiator Springs, Lightning interrupted Mater's story. "Whoa!" he cried. "What did you do?"

Mater looked over at his friend. "Don't you remember nothin'? We was a tag team."

Mater continued his story, except this time, Lightning was also in the ring, wearing his own flashy wrestling outfit. He nervously stared up at the Monster.

"TAG, YOU'RE IT!" said Mater, touching Lightning with his tire.

The Monster lunged for the race car, ignoring the tow truck.

"What?" Lightning was confused. Then he saw their opponent coming straight at him. **"AAAAHH!"** Lightning raced around the ring to avoid the Monster's wrecking ball.

Meanwhile, the Tormentor ducked out of the ring and started chatting with two fans. When he heard Lightning call for help, the Tormentor ducked back into the ring.

The Monster was determined to win. He dropped his
wrecking ball, just missing Lightning. The race car froze,
not sure where to go.

Luckily, the Tormentor had a plan.

While the Monster's wrecking ball was on the ground,
the Tormentor quickly snagged it with his tow hook.

"GOTCHA!" Then he zipped under one side of the ring and out the other.

With a wink at his fans, the Tormentor yanked his towline. He flipped the entire ring—trapping Dr. Frankenwagon and the Monster underneath!

"THE WINNERS!" the referee announced. "The Tormentor and . . ." He turned to Lightning. "What's your name, son?"

"Lightning McQueen," he replied.

"And Frightening McMean!" the ref declared.

Outside Flo's V8 Café, Lightning listened doubtfully to the end of Mater's story. Just then a fan rolled up and asked for the Tormentor's autograph.

"Don't you want Frightening McMean's autograph?" Lightning asked.

"No, thanks," the fan replied and drove away.

UFM

UNIDENTIFIED FLYING MATER

At Luigi's Casa Della Tires, his assistant, Guido, was putting a new hubcap on a customer. Suddenly the hubcab slipped! It bounced off a pole and smashed through the store's front window. The hubcap flew past Mater and Lightning McQueen, who were stopped at a traffic light outside.

"HEY, LOOK, A UFO!" Mater shouted. "And I know, 'cause I done seen one once," he told Lightning.

Then Mater began to tell his friend a tale about the time he saw a spaceship. "It was a crystal-clear night." Mater began his story. . . .

Mater pulled up to a railroad crossing in the desert. Suddenly clouds gathered overhead. Then the signals started flashing wildly, even though no train was in sight.

"THAT'S WEIRD," Mater muttered. He looked to the left. . . .

Nothing.

He looked to the right. . . .

Nothing.

Then Mater looked forward. "AAAAAH!"
A UFO was floating right in front of him!
"Well, hey there," he said. "Welcome. My name is Mater."
"My name is Mator," the UFO replied.
"Mator? Huh." That sounded an awful lot like his own name,
the tow truck thought. "Should I take you to my liter?"
"Your leader," the UFO echoed.
Mater rolled off with the UFO flying behind him.

Mater led the UFO to the spot where he kept his oil cans. "Here are all my liters," he said.

The UFO looked excited. "YUM!" he cried.

Mater grabbed a can and drank the oil through a straw. When he glanced over, the UFO was slurping from a large oil drum. But Mater didn't mind. He was always happy to share.

Then the UFO let out a belch. A really loud belch.
"DADGUM!" Mater said, impressed.
"Dadgum!" the UFO echoed.
Later, Mater showed his new friend around. They did all
Mater's favorite things, including tractor tipping.

After that, Mater taught the UFO how to drive backward.
Then his new friend taught Mater how to fly!
"WHOA!" the tow truck exclaimed.
Mater and the UFO went zipping through the night sky.

The UFO zoomed away, but Mater caught up as they rounded Willy's Butte. They were both having a great time.

"We're going to be best friends forever!" Mater said.

Out of nowhere, a giant magnet dropped from the night sky. *ZINGGGG!* It grabbed the UFO and pulled him upward. Three military helicopters were hovering overhead.

"I got him," one helicopter said.

"Return to base," another helicopter ordered.

"MATOR! I'LL SAVE YOU!" Mater
yelled as the helicopters left.
 Mater was determined to help his new friend. He
secretly followed the helicopters through the desert.
He passed a sign that read, NO TRESPASSING: PARKING AREA 51.

Mater followed the helicopters to a military base. He sneaked inside past the guards, and then he spotted a large airplane hangar. When he looked in a hangar window, Mater saw the UFO hanging from the huge magnet.

Several military and science vehicles were closely examining the UFO. A scientist snapped a photo of Mator using a bright flash.
"DADGUM!" the UFO exclaimed.

All the scientists seemed excited that the UFO had spoken.

"'Dadgum'?" one scientist repeated. "He's trying to communicate! Where's Dr. Abschleppwagen?"

Mater knew this was his chance. He quickly put on a scientist disguise, then burst into the room. "HERE I AM!" he announced.

"What does 'dadgum' mean?" asked one scientist.

Mater looked around and spotted a giant ON/OFF switch.

"It means . . ." he began. Then he threw the switch, turning off the magnet. "LET'S GET OUT OF HERE!"

The UFO was freed. "Dadgum!" he exclaimed.

"Follow me!" Mater shouted to his friend.

Mater and Mator flew out of the hangar at top speed.
Everyone from the military base chased after them. . . .
In Radiator Springs, Lightning interrupted Mater's story.
**"DO YOU REALLY EXPECT ME TO
BELIEVE THAT?"**

The tow truck shrugged. "You should," he said. "You was there, too!" Then he continued his story.

Except this time, Mater described how Lightning was zooming across the desert with him and Mator. All the military vehicles were close behind. Mater was afraid he and his friends wouldn't get away.

Suddenly, an enormous UFO mother ship appeared.

"Whoa!" Mater exclaimed.

"IT'S BEAUTIFUL!" Lightning said.

The mother ship pulled Mater, Mator, and Lightning aboard in a white beam of light. Then the ship blasted into space, leaving everyone else far behind.

"Dadgum!" all the military vehicles exclaimed.

After a quick ride through space, it was time for Mater and Lightning to get back.

"Thanks for saving us, Mrs. UFO," Mater said. "Can you drop us off at home?"

The mother ship stopped over Mater's shed and dropped him and Lightning right through the roof.

"Thank you!" Mater called. He would miss his new friend, Mator, but he was glad the little UFO was safe.

Outside the tire shop in Radiator Springs, Lightning looked skeptical. "I'm sorry, Mater," he said. "That did not happen."

"Oh, yeah?" Mater replied. "THEN HOW COME I CAN DO THIS?"

He tried to fly, but his gears started grinding loudly.

"Oh, Mater, please." Lightning rolled his eyes and drove away.

Finally, Mater rose into the air. With a laugh, he flew off into the clear blue sky.

It was a warm, sunny day in Radiator Springs, and Lightning McQueen and Mater were cruising through town. Red the fire truck was watering some flowers in front of the fire station. **"HEY, RED!"** Lightning called.

"I used to be a fire truck," Mater said, out of the blue.

"What?" Lightning exclaimed.

"Dadgum right," Mater replied.

Then he began to tell the story of Rescue Squad Mater....

Rescue Squad Mater was at the fire station when an emergency call came in.

"ALL UNITS! ALL UNITS!" shouted the dispatcher on the radio. "Fire in progress at one-two-zero-niner Car Michael Way."

Rescue Squad Mater gasped. He recognized that address.

"That's the old gasoline and match factory!" he exclaimed. Luckily he was gassed up and ready to roll.

"MATER ONE EN ROUTE!"

He knew he had to get to the factory—fast. He zoomed out of the station and roared down the street at top speed. Cars and trucks cleared the way to let him through. Mater was racing to the rescue!

Moments later, Rescue Squad Mater sped up to the burning building.

"BACK IT UP, FOLKS," a police trooper called to the crowd that had gathered to watch. "Make room for Mater!"

The rescue truck squealed to a stop in front of the blazing fire.

"We're counting on you!" the firehouse dispatcher said over the radio.

"I'M ON IT!" Rescue Squad Mater aimed a water hose and started spraying.

He bravely battled the flames, ignoring the danger. . . .

"Mater," Lightning said, interrupting the story, "I can't believe that you were a fire truck."

"You remember," Mater replied. "For Pete's sake, you were there, too!"

Then he went on telling his tale. . . .

The fire had spread through the entire factory, but Rescue Squad Mater still continued to battle it. Suddenly, a frightened voice called out.

"AAAH! HELP! HELP!" Lightning was stuck on the top floor of the burning building!

"Remain calm," Mater shouted to him.

"I GOTCHA!"

The rescue truck sprayed another blast of water to
beat back the flames. Then he began to raise his ladder
toward the top floor.

Rescue Squad Mater knew that he was the only one
who could help Lightning at that moment.

Soon the ladder was right beneath Lightning. Would there be enough time for Rescue Squad Mater to get him safely to the ground—before the factory exploded?

The crowd watched anxiously, waiting on the edges of their tire treads.

KA-BLAM!

The factory blew up in a huge explosion!

Luckily, by then Lightning was out of the building. Rescue Squad Mater had done it. He'd saved the day.

"Yay, Mater!" the onlookers cheered. "Awesome!"

Mater didn't have time to celebrate. He had to make sure his best friend wasn't hurt. He used his ladder to lift Lightning into an ambulance.

"THE HOSPITAL, STAT!" he ordered. "He's overheating."

"I got it!" the ambulance said, and then sped away.

Finally Mater turned toward the crowd and smiled.

When Lightning arrived at the hospital, a medic rushed him to the operating room.

The freshly scrubbed room was filled with medical equipment, such as battery chargers, grease guns, and some other tools that Lightning wasn't so sure about.

A whole team of nurses and assistants was there, too.
Lightning looked around. Where was the doctor?
Then he heard a nurse's voice over the loudspeaker.
"PAGING DR. MATER."
Lightning blinked. Had he heard that right?

Seconds later, the doctor rolled in. Lightning could hardly believe his eyes. It *was* Mater! He looked calm and professional in his surgical mask and headlamp.

"All righty, now," Dr. Mater told his patient. **"LET'S HAVE A LOOK-SEE."**

"Mater, you're a doctor, too?" Lightning asked in surprise.

"That's right, buddy," Dr. Mater replied. "Got my MD, my PhD, my STP, and my GTO."

Lightning spotted Dr. Mater's diplomas on the wall. What kind of a degree was a GTO? he wondered.

At that moment, a pretty nurse rolled into the room. She was wearing a jaunty cap, and the letters *GTO* were painted on her sides.

"HEY, DOCTOR," she said with a wink.

Dr. Mater smiled back. Then he got down to business.
He had a patient to save, and he took his job seriously.
"Clear!" he called out as he swung the arm of a
scary-looking medical instrument toward Lightning.
"AAAAHH!" Lightning screamed.

Then Mater stopped telling his story.

"Well?" Lightning asked. "What happened?"

"I SAVED YOUR LIFE," Mater said.

"Whaaa . . . ?" Lightning was pretty sure he would remember something like that. "No, you didn't!"

"Did so," Mater replied.

"Did not," Lightning insisted.

Then a yellow GTO drove by. "Hello, Doctor."

"Did so," Mater told Lightning smugly.

EL MATERDOR

One fine day in Radiator Springs, Mater and Lightning McQueen were out for a drive together. Lightning stopped to look at some grazing bulldozers.

"THEM'S JUST LIKE THE ONES I USED TO FIGHT," said Mater.

"What?" Lightning cried in disbelief.

"That's right," Mater replied. "I was a famous bulldozer fighter in Spain." He began to tell his tale.

"THEY CALLED ME 'EL MATERDOR,'" Mater went on,

spinning his story. He described his decked-out gold paint job.

As El Materdor stood in the center of a packed arena, he struck a confident pose. The crowd cheered wildly!

Among the fans in the stands were two Spanish senoritas. "Senor Materdor!" they called as they *oohed* and *aahed* over the famous bulldozer fighter. Just one wink from the brave El Materdor made his adoring fans gasp and giggle.

Soon it was time for business. With a nod of his head, El Materdor signaled that he was ready. A door at the side of the ring opened, and a giant, angry-looking bulldozer rolled out. For a while, the two vehicles stood, eyes locked, sizing each other up.

Finally El Materdor raised his tow hook. One glimpse of the red cape dangling from it and—**PRESTO!**—the bulldozer charged full-speed toward the cape.

El Materdor stood his ground, not moving an inch. Then, just in time, he whisked his cape out of the bulldozer's path.
"OLÉ!" the crowd cheered.

Again and again, the bulldozer charged. Each time, El Materdor dodged him with a last-second move. Until the bulldozer finally surprised him. He came up behind El Materdor and pushed him clear across the ring, driving him right into the ground!

The Spanish senoritas, along with the rest of the crowd, watched and waited in silence. COULD THIS BE THE END OF EL MATERDOR? He was completely buried.

Then the tow truck's hook poked out from a pile of dirt. At the end of it was El Materdor's red cape. The battle would go on!

El Materdor dusted himself off and bravely faced the huge bulldozer once again. They cruised slowly around the arena. Through narrowed eyes, they studied each other. The arena was silent except for the sound of their revving engines.

Suddenly, the bulldozer smacked his front blade on the ground. Two doors at the side of the ring opened and two more bulldozers drove out. NOW IT WAS THREE AGAINST ONE!

How in the world could El Materdor fight them all?

The bulldozers charged! For a time, El Materdor fought off all three of them. He used his backward-driving skills and showed off some other fancy moves. But then the three bulldozers circled him and began to close in.

There was nowhere for El Materdor to go. . . .

Nowhere but up, that is. El Materdor waited until the last possible moment. Then, with a mighty leap, he jumped clear out of the path of the charging bulldozers, who collided and collapsed in a twisted heap.

"OLÉ!" El Materdor cried, landing heroically on top of the wrecked bulldozers.

The crowd went wild! The adoring senoritas threw roses. El Materdor caught a flower in his grille, and the ladies giggled.

But the celebration was short-lived.

Soon more bulldozers rolled into the ring. It turned out
that the wrecked ones had some friends.
"THERE I WAS, SURROUNDED,"
Mater told Lightning. "Bulldozers all around me."

Mater and Lightning were still stopped in the middle of Radiator Springs. A fence separated them from the field of grazing bulldozers. Lightning was hanging on Mater's every word. "What did you do?" he asked.

"What did I . . . ?" Mater began. "Don't you remember? YOU WAS THERE, TOO!"

Then Mater continued his story, but this time he
included Lightning in the action. "They sure liked your
fancy red paint job," Mater remembered.

In the arena, Lightning gasped. His paint job was red—
just like El Materdor's cape! The bulldozers revved their
engines and began to chase Lightning around the ring.

"OLÉ!" the crowd cheered.

Back in Radiator Springs, Lightning interrupted the story. "Mater," he said, "that did not happen."

"Well, try telling that to them there bulldozers," Mater replied, pointing behind Lightning. The bulldozers that had been grazing on the other side of the fence were now surrounding Mater and Lightning!

"Huh?" Lightning noticed the bulldozers eyeing his shiny red paint job.

He took off down the dirt road, the bulldozers speeding after him.

Just then, two fans rolled up alongside Mater.
"Senor Mater," they said together.
"*Senoriters*," Mater replied charmingly. He tossed
on a matador hat. "OLÉ!"

It was a warm night in Radiator Springs. All the cars had gathered at Flo's V8 Café for karaoke.

Guido sang "Camptown Races." Unfortunately, no one but Luigi could understand him, because he was singing in Italian!

Lightning McQueen looked over at Mater. "Why don't you get up there and sing?" he asked his friend.

"Nah, I don't want to steal the show," Mater replied.

Lightning was confused. "'Steal the show'?"

"WELL, I WAS A BIG ROCK STAR,"

Mater said, grinning.

"What?" Lightning couldn't believe what he was hearing.

Mater began to tell a story about the time he was in a rock group. "I started out in a garage band...."

Mater described how his rock band, Mater and the Gas-Caps, would rehearse in a garage. He was the lead singer, and pitties played the drums, electric guitar, and bass guitar.

"DADGUM, DADGUM, DAAADGUM," Mater sang into a microphone.

When the song came to an end, Mater said, "Boy, we sound pretty good."

The pitties agreed.

"LET'S GET A GIG!" Mater suggested.

Soon Mater and the Gas-Caps had a gig at the
Top-Down Truck Stop. The band performed for a line of
semitrucks who were fueling up. Waitresses drove around
serving the trucks cans of oil.

When the band finished, the trucks cheered.

"That so rocked!" exclaimed a waitress named Mia.

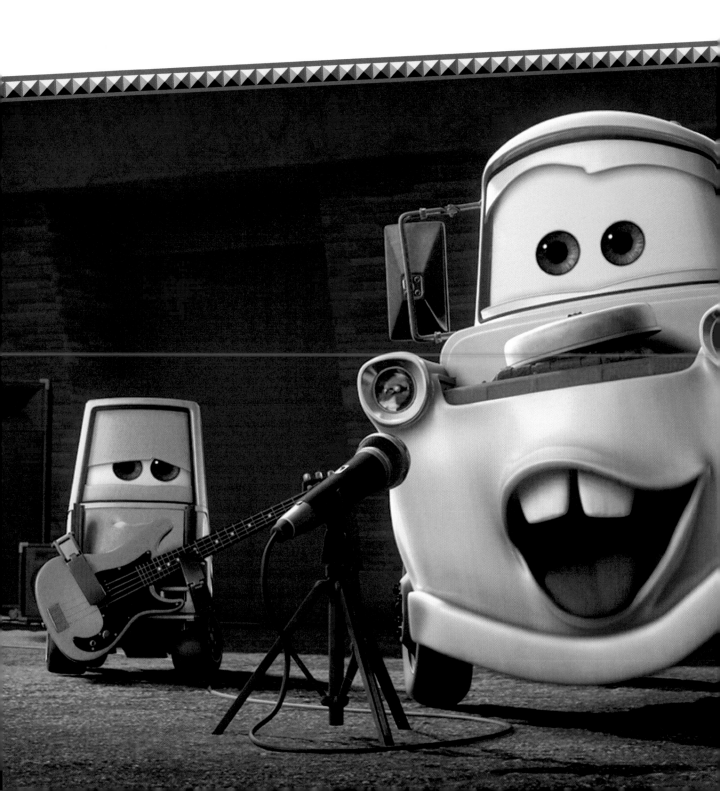

"I know!" agreed another named Tia.
"DO YOU GUYS HAVE A RECORD?"
Mia and Tia asked the band.

The guitar player shook his head, but Mater smiled. He had an idea.

Not long after, Mater and the Gas-Caps were in a recording studio. Everyone in the band performed their song the best they could.

"DADGUM, DADGUM, DADGUM, dadgum, dadgum, dadgum, *daaaaad*gum," sang Mater.

In the middle of recording the song, a fly buzzed around the drummer. The pittie waved it away.

"SHOO! SHOO!" he cried, blowing at it.

But the fly kept zooming around his head. The pittie tried to hit the fly using a drumstick. As he wildly swung at the insect, he banged on the drums faster and faster!

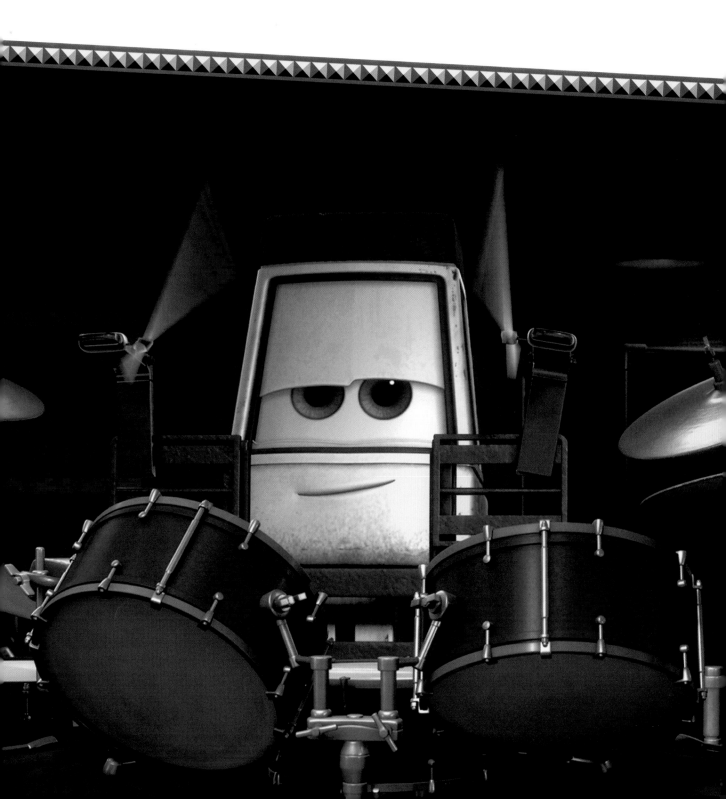

The guitar pittie strummed more, trying to keep up with the drummer's beat.

Mater gasped. What was going on with his band? He began singing faster and louder.

After a few seconds, he realized he liked the new sound. **"OH, YEAH! WHEE-HOO!"** he shouted. "Dadgum, dadgum, dadgum, dadgum!!!"

Mater sang so loudly that everyone in the recording studio heard him. Doors began to open. Cars peeked out. **"WHAT'S THAT SOUND?"** someone wondered aloud.

A music agent named Dex knew the answer. "Sounds like angels printing money to me!" He liked the song.

Dex rolled into Mater's recording booth.

"Dadgum, *daaad!*" Mater sang. Then, just like a true rock star, he kicked down the microphone with his back tire.

"SAY, YOU BOYS ARE GOOD," Dex told the band. Then he noticed their name on the drums. "All you need is a new name."

"'A new name'?" repeated Mater. He tried to think of one, but nothing came to mind.

At that moment, a delivery pittie entered the studio. "Where do you want this heavy metal, Mater?" he asked.

"THAT'S IT!" cried Mater. That was the band's new name!

Heavy Metal Mater was an overnight success. They packed stadiums and had thousands of fans. The concerts they gave were instant sellouts. Word had spread quickly about their amazing stage performances. They used lots of lights and even had fiery explosions.

Center stage at one of their shows, Mater rocked out. "Dadgum and dadgum and dadgum and dadgum . . ."

"DADGUM!" repeated the audience.

Suddenly, a giant Mater balloon with wings lifted up from behind the stage. It began to float over the audience. The crowd went wild!

In Radiator Springs, Lightning interrupted the story. "You were Heavy Metal Mater?"

"No," the tow truck replied. "*We* was Heavy Metal Mater!"

Then he continued his tale. Except this time Lightning was in the band, too.

Mater described how he was onstage at the concert. Then a platform rose up. Lightning was on it, wearing sunglasses.

"ARE YOU READY TO ROCK?!" Lightning yelled. Then he jumped down and joined Mater.

"DADGUM! DADGUM!" Mater
and Lightning sang together.

At Flo's V8 Café, Lightning interrupted again.

"I'm sorry," he said with a laugh, "that did not happen." **"WELL, SUIT YOURSELF,"** Mater replied, motioning to the sky.

Lightning looked up. The balloon from the concert was flying overhead! Had Mater been telling the truth?

MATER
★ ★ ★ ★ THE ★ ★ ★ ★
GREATER

Lightning McQueen and his friends were enjoying a few oil cans at Flo's V8 Café when . . .

"WHOA!"

Mater sped backward over a ramp. He zoomed through the air and crashed into a pile of cans.

"Mater, are you all right?" Lightning asked.

"Well, of course, I'm all right," the tow truck replied. "I used to be a daredevil."

Lightning wasn't sure whether to believe him or not.

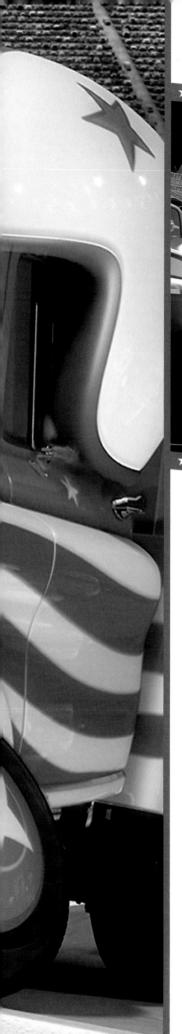

"Folks would come from all around to see my stunts." Mater began to tell the story of his days as a daredevil. He described the stars-and-stripes paint job he had as Mater the Greater. One of his events was at a packed sports arena. There were spotlights, photographers, and reporters.

"Ladies and gentlecars . . ." the announcer called, "Mater the Greater!"

In the stands, fans waved signs and cheered.

"GET YOUR MATER TEETH RIGHT HERE!" a salesman shouted as he walked the aisles. "Two buckteeth for one buck!"

Many of the fans were already wearing their souvenirs.

A spotlight followed Mater the Greater as he rolled down a launching ramp. The cheering crowd quieted. It was nearly time for Mater's big stunt. He would try to jump over an incredibly long line of cars!

MATER THE GREATER

MATER THE GREATER

Mater the Greater began to back up. He would
need lots of room to speed up enough to make it over
all the cars. He rolled to the very edge of the arena.
Finally, with his back tires against the barrier,

MATER WAS SET TO GO.

"AND HE'S OFF!" the announcer called out.

Mater's wheels burned rubber as he drove toward the ramp. He sped faster and faster, knocking over orange safety cones and blowing off photographers' hats as he rocketed past.

Cameras flashed around the stadium. This was it! Every car in the place held their breath as they watched and wondered: **WOULD MATER MAKE IT?**

Mater the Greater raced up the ramp, launched off the end, and then . . .

THUD! Mater the Greater landed on the first two cars past the ramp.

"*Oww!*" one car cried.

"*Oooh! Owww . . .*" Each car in the lineup groaned as Mater the Greater tiptoed all the way down the row.

"'Scuse me!" he said. "Pardon me! Comin' through!"

At last, Mater the Greater rolled over the last car. He scooted down the ramp on the other side.

"HE DID IT!" the announcer cried.

The crowd went wild! Mater the Greater had made his way over all the cars. It didn't matter to them how he had done it.

"I DID ALL KINDS OF STUNTS,"

Mater told Lightning as he continued his story. He described being shot from a cannon through a ring of flames! The stunt ended in a huge explosion. Mater the Greater caught fire and had to be put out with a fire extinguisher. But the audience loved it anyway.

Another time, Mater the Greater was riding on the wing
of an airplane. Everything was going fine until the stunt
plane did a few rolls, turning upside down! Mater the
Greater slipped off the plane and began to fall. He quickly
released his tow hook and caught it on the plane's wheel. He
finished the ride dangling from the plane by his towline.

In another daredevil stunt, Mater the Greater dove
from a superhigh platform into a tiny pool of water.
Amazingly, he landed right on target, although he split
the pool wide open. And that's not all that broke!
**"I DONE BUSTED NEARLY EVERY
PART OF MY BODY,"** Mater remembered.

"The biggest stunt Mater the Greater ever did was jumping Carburetor Canyon," Mater told Lightning.

Mater described how even with a giant ramp and a rocket strapped to his hood, the jump seemed impossible.

Lightning was starting to doubt the story. "Jumping Carburetor Canyon?" he asked. **"NO WAY."**

"YES, WAY," Mater replied. "You remember. You was there, too." He continued his story, except now Lightning was with him.

Lightning had a fancy new paint job, and three huge rockets were strapped to his roof. He even had on Mater the Greater souvenir teeth!

"Ready, buddy?" Mater the Greater asked. But Lightning didn't really have a chance to answer. One of the pitties lit his rockets and pushed him down the ramp!

"AND THERE HE GOES!" an announcer's voice echoed through the canyon.

Lightning shot down the ramp and launched into the air.

Lightning was about halfway across the canyon when his rockets sputtered . . . and went out.

By this time, everyone at Flo's V8 Café was listening. They were all waiting to hear the end of Mater's story.

"WELL, WHAT HAPPENED?" Lightning asked.

"You didn't make it," Mater replied. "Well, see ya later!"

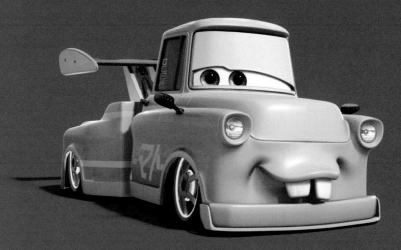

Tokyo Mater

One afternoon, Mater, Sheriff, and Lightning McQueen stopped for oil at Flo's V8 Café. Suddenly, three flashy modified cars roared past them.

"Get back here, you import punks!" yelled Sheriff. He took off after them.

"I USED TO BE AN IMPORT,"

Mater said.

"What? No way!" Lightning exclaimed.

"Yes, way," Mater replied. He began to tell a story. "It all started one day. . . ."

Mater described to Lightning how he was driving through Carburetor County and saw an older car sitting on the side of the road. Mater pulled up.

"Looks like you could use a tow somewhere," he said.

"It is very far," replied the older car. His name was Ito-san.

"Well, no tow is too far for Tow Mater!" exclaimed Mater.

Mater towed Ito-san all the way to Tokyo!
He came out of the Sea of Japan gasping for air. "MAN,
I GOTTA CHANGE MY SLOGAN!"
Mater unhooked Ito-san and looked around. "Whoa!" Mater
had never seen so many tall buildings before.

143

Then Mater rolled backward and accidentally bumped into Kabuto, the leader of a gang of ninja cars.

"You scratched my paint," Kabuto snarled. He circled around Mater, his tires kicking up a big cloud of smoke. **"DORIFUTO DE SHOUBU DA!"** he said in Japanese.

"What-sa?" asked Mater.

"He challenges you to a drift race." Ito-san explained that in a drift race, a car drives fast and steers hard into turns. That type of driving makes the car slide on the road.

"We will race at midnight," Kabuto said, then sped away.

"YOU NEED MODIFICATION," Ito-san said.
With help from some other cars, Mater soon got a slick blue paint job and a large rear spoiler. At midnight, he pulled up to the starting line next to Kabuto.

"Race to the top of Tokyo Tower. First one to seize the flag will become King of All Drifters," Ito-san explained.

"What happens to the loser?" asked Mater.

"The loser will be stripped of all modifications and become stock," Kabuto said with a wicked grin.

"But I just got all this fancy stuff!" said Mater. He didn't want to lose his new paint job.

"READY . . . SET . . . GO!"

Kabuto and Mater peeled out, zipping through the streets. Kabuto steered around sharp corners and drifted at high speeds. He was in the lead! Mater tried to catch up. But he was driving so fast that he missed a turn.

"You can't drift! Ha-ha-ha!" Kabuto laughed.

"I'll show you!" Mater declared.

Instead, Mater accidentally went the wrong direction
on a one-way street.

"Get back here, you import punk!" a police officer
called. He turned on his siren and followed Mater.

The tow truck drove into a donut shop. Inside, cop cars
were making donut shapes by driving in circles.

"I love donuts!" the officer said and started spinning.

Mater sped away down an alley. He saw Kabuto up ahead, and drove up next to him.

"Good," said Kabuto. "But not good enough. Ninjas, attack!"

A group of ninjas suddenly appeared and surrounded Mater. He was forced to slow down while Kabuto sped off. "OH, NO! NINJAS!" cried Mater.

Back in Radiator Springs, Lightning was shocked by this part of Mater's story.

"WHAT DID YOU DO?" he asked.

"Well, shoot. You oughta know," Mater replied. "You was there, too!"

Then Mater continued telling his story, except now Lightning was part of the adventure.

Mater described how he was surrounded by ninjas.
Suddenly, a bolt of lightning shot down. When the smoke cleared, Dragon Lightning McQueen was there. "I'll take care of this—dragonstyle!" he said.

"*EEEE!*" cried the ninjas.

With a kick of his rear tire, Lightning sent each ninja flying through the air. *"Ka-chow!"*

Then Lightning and Mater sped down the highway.

Mater spotted Kabuto in the distance. "Oh, no! He's almost to the tower."

"Quickly, follow me!" cried Lightning.

"Right behind ya!" Mater replied.

Mater and Lightning jumped onto a construction site. A
giant crane woke up and accidentally knocked over a row
of oil cans. Oil splashed all over the road! The cars were
going so fast, they slid across the slippery surface.

"*Wheee!* Look at me!" exclaimed Mater.
"I'M DRIFTING!"

Then Mater saw the end of the construction site ahead.

"I can't stop!" he shouted. The oil was too slick.

Lightning pushed Mater into a huge pipe and used his flame thrower to light some oil on the ground. *KA-BOOM!* The oil exploded and the tow truck launched into the air.

"Cannonball!" Mater yelled as he flew over the city.

Meanwhile, Kabuto was nearly to Tokyo Tower.
"VICTORY IS MINE," he said.

Just then, Mater landed in front of him. "Well, hey!"
Mater shouted. He took off down the highway, driving
backward. Kabuto chased after him.

Soon they reached the road that led to the top of
Tokyo Tower.

Mater drove backward up the narrow road and wouldn't let Kabuto pass.

"YOU CANNOT DEFEAT ME!" Kabuto said.

"I can, too! Can, too! Can, too!" Mater called.

Then Kabuto pushed Mater over the railing. Mater quickly threw his tow hook onto the tower and pulled himself up to the top. He had finished the race first!

"I win!" Mater said proudly.

Afterward, Mater celebrated his victory with a big party.
Kabuto was stripped of his modifications and became a
plain, boring car. His ninja gang found another leader.

In Radiator Springs, Mater finished his story with: "That's
how I became Tokyo Mater, King of all the Drifters."

The sun was shining brightly in Radiator Springs. Lightning McQueen drove up to the gas station. "Can I get some air?" he called. "My tires are going flat."

Just then, Mater popped up as if out of nowhere. "Flat tires, ya say? I thought I done solved that crime."

"What?" asked Lightning, confused.

"I WAS A PRIVATE EYE," Mater
explained proudly.

"No way!" Lightning said.

"Yes, way!" replied Mater. Then he started to tell his
friend a story about his detective days. "It was seven
fifteen on a Friday night . . ." he began.

Mater sat behind the desk in his office. On the door was a sign that read: MATER, PRIVATE INVESTIGATOR. Mater was reading a newspaper article about several accidents, which were caused by tires blowing out.

"I was on to something real big," Mater explained. "There was some kind of counterfeit-tire ring."

KNOCK, KNOCK!

A car named Tia drove in. She was wearing a black veil and whitewall tires. "I need you to find my sister, Mia," cried Tia.

"SHE'S BEEN CARNAPPED!"

"Where did you last see her?" asked Mater.

"She was working for Big D at his club," said Tia. "The Carbacabana."

Big D was a fancy sedan who had recently opened a new nightclub.

That night, Mater went to the Carbacabana.

Onstage, a singer named Carmen was performing with her band. Mater suspected she knew what had happened to Mia. Carmen and Mia had worked together at the club.

After her song, Carmen came over to Mater's table.

"I'm looking for Mia. Have you seen her?" Mater asked.

"THAT RAGTOP!" exclaimed Carmen. "I don't remember."

Mater didn't believe her. So he placed four new whitewall tires on the table.

Suddenly, Carmen remembered. "I saw her a couple of days ago with Big D. She smelled salty, like the ocean."

Before Mater could ask any more questions, two mean forklifts named Clyde and Claude threw him out of the club. They dragged him into a back alley.

"You know what happens to guys who shine their headlights in the wrong places?" Claude asked Mater.

"THEY LOSE 'EM!"

Claude took out one of Mater's headlights and smashed it on the ground. It was a warning not to mess with Big D.

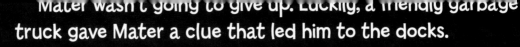

Mater wasn't going to give up. Luckily, a friendly garbage truck gave Mater a clue that led him to the docks.

Then he saw Mia on the deck of a huge cargo boat! She was wearing a cement boot to prevent her from escaping.

Mater hid inside a crate and tried to sneak onto the boat to rescue her.

At that moment, the crate lifted up. Mater had been spotted!

Some dockworkers surrounded Mater. Then
Big D rolled out. A crane grabbed Mater and
hoisted him up.

Just then, Tia rushed forward. **"NO!"**

Mater was angry. Tia had told Big D that
Mater would come to the docks. "You double-
crossing double-crosser!" shouted Mater.

Tia explained that it was the only way to
save her sister.

"Well, you always did the right thing . . . just
the wrong way," Mater said as the crane pulled
him over the water.

Back in Radiator Springs, Lightning was on the edge of his bumper.
"WHAT DID YOU DO?" he asked.

Mater laughed aloud. "Like you don't know, Lieutenant Lightning McQueen!"

Then Mater continued telling his tale. Except this time, his friend was in the story, too.

Police Lieutenant Lightning McQueen drove onto the docks with a group of squad cars. "Looks like we finally caught you, Big D," he said.

"GET HIM!" a dockworker shouted. The workers pushed barrels down the boat ramp to keep the police away.

Meanwhile, Tia was trying to rescue Mater. She hit a
switch on the crane, and it lowered Mater to the ground.
Then Mater threw his tow hook at another crane.
CRASH! The crane dropped its crate—right on Big D!

The crate split open, and tires spilled all over Big D.
"Aha! Just what I thought—counterfeit tires," Mater said.
Big D had been swapping good tires for fake ones. It was his
fault there had been so many car accidents lately.

Now that Mater had uncovered Big D's scam, the police stepped in.

"You led us right to him, Mater," Lightning announced gratefully. "Take him away, boys!"

Lightning's men surrounded Big D and led him off the docks toward the police station.

Tia rolled up next to Mater.
"THAT WAS A FINE MESS YOU GOT ME INTO, TIA," Mater said.
"I'm not bad," she told him. "I just drive that way."
Tia turned to look at Mater, but he was already gone! He'd had enough trouble for one day.

Back in Radiator Springs, Lightning was laughing. "Mater, that is the most ridiculous thing I've ever heard!" he said.

Suddenly, Carmen rolled up. "Come on!" she called. **"EVERYBODY, CONGA!"**

Carmen's band was following her in a conga line. Mater joined them and started dancing.

Lightning's mouth hung open as he watched Mater and the band dance down the street.